# THE RELUCTANT ANGEL

## THE SECRET EVEN YOUR ANGEL DOESN'T KNOW

MARIA MCSHANE

To Spencer,
All my best,
Maria McShane

*To Danny, my heart still breaks and cries for you. Thank you for reuniting with me here.*

# I

MayBea, the elderly bulldog, lay panting in her bed. Her body ached, the pressure on her chest excruciating with every breath. Her owners, Maryah and Lars, hovered close. The cool touch of their hands comforted her.

"Oh, my sweet dog," Maryah cried. "Please don't go."

MayBea's eyes fluttered open, and she stared at what her humans could not see. Her canine spirit guide and ancestor, Goliath, lingered nearby. He waited to escort her Home.

"Uhh, uhhmm," MayBea grunted. "How will she find her way without me? I must stay."

Maryah pulled her close and sobbed into her fur. Lars wrapped them both in his arms, hands trembling. Together, they were a family again. Moments such as this had been sparse for some time.

"Uhh, uhhmm." MayBea leaned against them. "My work is not finished."

She gazed at where Goliath sat. He raised his head as if

to grant consent. The agony eased as if he shouldered the burden of it.

Invigorated, MayBea sat up and licked Maryah's cheek.

"Look, honey," Maryah said. "MayBea is doing better. She's not ready to go."

MayBea grunted, shook it off, and trotted to her food dish.

"She's better for now," Lars said in disbelief.

"She's even hungry," Maryah exclaimed.

MayBea glanced at Goliath and nudged the dish. "Yes, I am better. I must eat."

The dream started as it had many times. There had been a fresh snowfall, the best for sledding. Snow crunched beneath her boots as Maryah trudged the familiar path through the snow to the frozen pond. Her ice skates knotted together and slung over her shoulder. Maryah and her brother, Danny, pulled their baby sister, Melody, on a Flying V sled.

"C'mon, hurry up," six-year-old Melody demanded.

"We'll get you there, kid," Danny said. "We're going as fast as we can."

Maryah glanced back to where Melody sat on the sled. She wore matching pink boots, a scarf, gloves, and a hat, her brown hair showing. Older than Melody by two and three years, she and Danny spoiled their youngest sibling.

"You're horses," Melody giggled. "Pulling me on my sleigh."

"OK, neigh, neigh," Maryah whinnied. "Silly kid."

"Giddyup." Melody tugged on make-believe reins.

"We're almost there," Danny announced.

"I can see the pond," Maryah said.

"C'mon, horsies, c'mon," Melody called. "We're going to have the best time ever."

They stopped at the pond where Maryah would join the older kids for ice skating. Danny and Melody would get in a few runs on the nearby sledding hill.

"I want to skate today," Melody pouted.

"We're going sliding," Danny said. "You're too little for skating."

Melody raised her chin, the pink knit ties of her hat bobbing under her chin. "No," she said, and crossed her arms.

The wind picked up the snow and dusted it around them. Maryah exchanged a look with Danny. When Mellie got bratty, there was no convincing her otherwise.

"You need to wait until next year," Maryah reasoned. Their mother had decreed that her children were not allowed on ice skates until they were seven.

"Let me try your skates," Mellie whined.

"They're too big for you," Maryah sighed. Being the older sibling, she had responsibility for her impulsive baby sister. If only their oldest brother, Tommy, was there. He had more success in getting Melody to mind.

"I want to skate," Mellie repeated. "Just for a little while."

"You know she won't stop until we let her," Danny said.

Maryah glanced at where Danny stood in his gray jacket, black boots, and gloves. "Just five minutes. You hold my hand and do what I tell you," she relented.

"Yay, I'm going to skate," Mellie sang. "Help me put them on."

Maryah held Melody's pink mittened hand in hers and led her to the old log the kids sat on to put their skates on. The pond wasn't as crowded today, just a handful of kids skating across the ice.

Danny sat beside Melody and removed one of her boots, while Maryah kneeled and helped her with the other.

"I'm going to be an ice princess," Melody chirped.

"You stay with us," Maryah directed, and laced up the skates. She glanced toward the edge of the clearing near the trees. "I'll be right back." She pointed.

"You have to wee-wee?" Melody asked.

"Stop, silly," Maryah said.

"Wee-wee, wee-wee," Melody chimed.

Danny and Melody broke up in laughter.

Maryah ignored them and headed for the trees and privacy. She'd just finished and was ready to return when the screams echoed across the clearing. She launched into a run, heart racing.

"Melody," she screamed.

When she reached the pond, at the far edge where the ice was the thinnest, she could see someone had fallen through. The big kids stood nearby, looking scared as hell. The top of Melody's pink hat was visible, bobbing above the water. Danny kneeled at the opening in the ice. Together, they grabbed her jacket and tried to pull her out.

"Help us," Maryah screamed.

The older kids made a daisy chain and helped drag Melody out. She lay on her back, icy wet, eyes closed, lips blue.

Maryah woke up next to her husband, Lars. She reached out and touched his shoulder. Her intent was not to wake him, but to confirm his presence and chase out the shadows of the past. Instead of Melody's singsong laughter in her head, Maryah heard the screams.

# 2

The next day, Maryah sat in her friend's backyard and stretched her legs, savoring the sun's warmth. Mid-November in Southern California, and the temperature was still mild. The dream weighed on her. She hadn't had it for some time.

The patio door opened, and her friend, Connie, emerged from the house carrying two glasses of iced tea. Connie had been raising English Bulldogs for thirty years under her kennel, Donaldson's Dynamo Bulldogs.

In her early sixties, Connie was a well-respected breeder by her contemporaries. In typical manner, she whistled Mary Had a Little Lamb, and her dogs trailed her, MayBea among them.

Maryah shook her head, managing a smile. "Only three days ago, I was afraid we might lose her," she said. "She still follows you like a little puppy."

Connie placed a glass before her, navigating the havoc the puppies and dogs created before sitting across from her. She hoisted a puppy onto her lap, pulled a tissue from her pocket, and wiped the puppy's eyes.

Maryah smiled and marveled at her friend's bond with all her dogs. They'd researched breeders when she and Lars decided to get an English Bulldog twelve years earlier. Connie's kennel had been renowned for champion dogs with a refined temperament.

MayBea was a gorgeous bulldog with a sweet disposition, a bit spoiled, and Maryah's universe. She was a brindle bulldog, brown and white, with a matching brown patch over each eye. The dog often drew attention whenever people saw her.

"Once a Donaldson dog, always a Donaldson dog," Connie stated. "And you're like the daughter I never had."

Since getting MayBea as a puppy, Maryah drove thirty miles every other week to visit her friend. Connie had become more like a mother to her since her own had passed ten years earlier.

"Thank you," Maryah said, holding her glass in mock salute. She gazed at the amber liquid, the same color as her favorite, honey-flavored whiskey. She swirled it before taking a quick gulp. If only she could banish the craving. The past six months sober had been her longest stretch.

Connie patted one of the dogs that nuzzled her leg. "What's going on?"

"It's just getting to be that time of year," Maryah paused. "The holidays."

"It can be hard for folks," Connie agreed.

"I've been thinking about Melody," Maryah exhaled. "It's coming up on the anniversary that we lost her."

"You'll never forget losing your baby sister," Connie

said. "But don't use it as an excuse to drown your sorrows and throw away the present."

Maryah rested her head on her chin, contemplating her friend's words. "I realize I used anything and everything as a reason to drink," she said.

"It wasn't easy for Harry when he quit," Connie spoke of her late husband. "You lose your crutch for coping. It's called living life on life's terms."

MayBea picked up a toy two puppies had been sharing and trotted to where Maryah sat. She laid down and held it between her paws.

"Such a diva," Maryah laughed, grateful for the distraction.

The puppies ran up and attempted to reclaim their prize. MayBea gave a warning growl.

"MayBea Donaldson, you stop that now," Connie declared.

MayBea sat up and relinquished the toy to the puppies.

"Good girl," Maryah patted her on the head.

MayBea rubbed her head against Maryah's leg, prompting to be scratched behind the ear.

"I know I've told you how much I love this dog," Maryah whispered. "She's given us so much joy. I wish she could last forever."

"It's the hardest thing a pet owner ever has to face," Connie acknowledged. "It doesn't get easier."

"I know," Maryah blinked hard.

"How are things with Lars?" Connie asked after a long silence.

"OK," Maryah murmured.

"Just OK?" Connie persisted.

Maryah wiped away a tear. "I've been moody, snapping at him. I don't know why."

"Have you been getting to meetings?" Connie asked.

"Yes. Even when I don't want to go, I do." Maryah confirmed her attendance at the twelve-step self-help meetings that had proven crucial in her quest to stay sober. Connie had been essential in guiding her to them.

"You've got a good fella there." The older woman reached out and touched her hand. "I've got twenty years on you. Don't make my mistakes. We forget to let those closest to us know we need and love them."

Maryah shifted in the chair. "I hate it when you're right," she said.

"I didn't mean to shut Harry out," Connie replied. "But I did. We never talked about Goliath after it happened. I froze him out. Harry started drinking more."

Maryah gazed at her friend, knowing the difficulty of the admission. "You've never told me much about Goliath," she said in a quiet voice.

"Goliath was the finest bulldog I ever had. He's the one that stole my heart, just like MayBea has yours." Connie removed her glasses and ran a hand through her short, gray hair. "But long before he was born, I loved another pet dearly. The one that I loved more than anything."

"Who was that?" Maryah wondered.

Connie reached down for one of the puppies and busied herself with it. "Billy," she said at last. "My pet goat."

"You had a pet goat?"

"When I was a kid," Connie answered, sipping her tea.

"We lived in a rural area with chickens, dogs, cats, a cow, and Billy. He followed me everywhere."

"As all your dogs do now," Maryah interjected.

"A lot like that," Connie smiled. "I would've brought Billy into the house if my mother had allowed it. My brothers built him a pen right outside my bedroom. I spent every waking moment with him."

"That's so cute." Maryah smiled, envisioning a young Connie chattering away to a pet goat. "How old were you?"

"Eight. My brothers were eleven and twelve," she replied. "He'd play games with all us kids. We'd play Hide and Seek. Billy would come and find me."

"Very cool," Maryah said.

Connie folded her arms. "My father wasn't crazy about him," she said.

Maryah sat silent. Connie seldom spoke of her past; this was the first time she'd mentioned her father.

"One day, Billy escaped from his pen and showed up at school," Connie continued. "He disrupted the class by 'baaing' outside until I brought him home. After, the teacher called my folks."

"What happened?" Maryah asked.

"Harry wasn't the only alcoholic in my life." Connie bent and patted the puppy that chewed on her shoes. She stared at where two dogs slept, their raspy snores filling the air. "At dinner that night, my father knocked us around, screaming we better find a way to keep Billy home."

Maryah regarded her friend. From what she knew, Harry didn't drink until the later years and had been a mellow, quiet drunk.

"I'm sorry," she said and hung her head. "I feel like a

jerk for telling you my crap about being an ass to my husband when I drink too much."

"We all have our baggage, honey. Reasons why we do what we do," Connie said. "I went to counseling after we got Goliath back. It helped us patch things up as best we could."

Maryah picked up an errant puppy that refused to stop chewing on her shoe. The puppy then opted for her finger. "Ouch," Maryah said. She touched the tip of his nose and kissed him on the head. "What about Billy?" she asked.

Connie tapped a finger on the table. "The next day, my brother secured him in the barn."

"Did he get out?" Maryah asked.

"No, he didn't," Connie said. "On our way home from school, we walked by the neighbor's, Jared Dennison. A mean bastard and drinking buddy of my father's. Bobby stopped, pushed me behind him, then screamed bloody murder."

The puppy in Maryah's arms squirmed and yipped. She placed him on the ground and waited.

Connie reached for a cigarette, lit it, and took a drag. "I squeezed around Bobby and saw Billy hanging from a tree in the front yard, blood draining. Dennison was holding a butcher's knife. He said our father sold Billy to him because he was a damn nuisance." Connie's voice trailed off. "A damn nuisance."

"Oh, my goodness." Maryah shuddered at the mental image. Her mouth felt dry. "How awful." She took a large gulp of tea.

Connie shook her head. "We got home and started screaming at the old man. He took his belt off, trying to hit us. Bobby and I jumped on him. We didn't care what he did. He knocked me to the ground, but I got right back up, kicking him."

Maryah held her breath and remained silent.

"My mother came out and fired the shotgun into the air, ending the ruckus," Connie said in a monotone. "The old man disappeared for a few days. That's the last time he ever hit us."

"Holy crap," Maryah said. "That's unbelievable." Her gut kicked at her friend's revelation. She leaned down and patted MayBea.

"That changed everything." Connie narrowed her gaze. "Even raising dogs, I loved them all, but never like Billy, until Goliath. Then I lost him too because of a drunk."

"But you said Goliath came home," Maryah said.

"He was gone for five years until we got him back," Connie explained.

MayBea stood and walked over to Connie and pressed against her leg.

Connie scratched her head. "Oh, you're my beautiful girl. What do you want, sweetie?" she asked. "To hear about Goliath?"

MayBea grunted.

"Looks like she remembers Goliath," Maryah commented.

"MayBea came many years after Goliath." Connie corrected, then turned to one of the dogs digging around a bush. "Hey, get outta there," she yelled.

The dog paused but resumed digging.

"Avocado, come here," Connie called.

Maryah laughed at the antics. Avocado stood fixated on her quest and ignored her.

Connie picked up a spray bottle of water, walked over,

and spritzed Avocado. "C'mon, doggies, let's go inside," she commanded, then began whistling Mary Had a Little Lamb.

Avocado backed away from the bush and turned. The other dogs and puppies tagged along behind her toward the house. MayBea followed suit.

Maryah laughed, savoring the sight of her dear friend trailed by bulldogs and puppies. "It doesn't get much better," she murmured and headed in after them.

"Do you want anything?" Connie asked once they were inside. She sat on a recliner sofa, two bulldogs on either side of her, another in a doggy bed nearby, a puppy in her lap. "Help yourself."

"I'm fine," Maryah responded and stood before a wall with photos of Connie's champion bulldogs taken over the years. "Which one is Goliath?"

"That one," Connie pointed. "That's when he won Best in Show, giving him enough points to finish as a champion."

Maryah touched one of the frames.

"Yes, that's him," Connie confirmed.

A younger Connie in a photo dated twenty years earlier stared at her. Still tall and thin, she kneeled beside a fawn-colored dog. Her hair was still in the same short style: dark brown, not gray. She stood with the dog posed in typical fashion after winning a show. Goliath was a bulky, handsome dog.

"He's gorgeous," Maryah murmured.

"The sweetest dog I ever had," Connie said. "He was something special."

# 3

MayBea lumbered over to where Connie sat. The aches and pain of the past few days had subsided. She knew it was due to the pills Lars and Maryah gave her throughout the day. "Pain med," is what they called it. But what caught her attention was the mention of Goliath. Her Goliath and Connie's were the same.

She observed the other dogs and pups, and Goliath was not among them. He only appeared to her when she'd been home with Maryah and Lars. Today, when Connie referenced him, she knew it was time to share his story with her pack.

One of the puppies came up and leaned against MayBea, snuggling against her.

MayBea grunted. "Listen, young one. I shall tell you of our ancestor, who waits for me and will be there for you."

Avocado sauntered over and then barked. The other dogs joined them.

"I will tell you, since my time is coming to an end. I shall pass on the story of Goliath. I will tell it as I have heard it," MayBea began. "Many years ago, before I came into the world, when our owner lady, Connie, was younger . . ."

Connie and Harry had been raising English Bulldogs for a few years. Connie's mentors, two longtime bulldoggers, claimed she was a natural after having already produced three champions. She had the heart and love for the breed. Goliath was the largest from their most recent litter of pups.

Goliath stole her heart from the moment she first held him in a way no pet had since childhood. The litter thrived, and two of the pups sold for top dollar. They made a small profit and enough to cover the vet costs, meds, and supplies.

"I'm keeping Magnolia and Goliath," Connie said of the two remaining pups. "He's my boy."

Connie showed the dogs and earned enough points in the ring to finish both as champions. Other litters came but without the success of Goliath's. Harry had lost his job. Growing bills and Harry's upcoming surgery necessitated Connie's return to work.

It was a Friday evening, and she was getting ready to work the night shift. Jonas Anderson, an acquaintance who had dabbled in bulldog breeding, dropped by.

He held a pizza and a six-pack. "Thought we'd watch the game," he said.

"C'mon in." Harry waved him in, and the two men exchanged a handshake.

Connie cleared space on the counter, handing Harry

paper plates and napkins. She nodded at Jonas. "Thanks for bringing dinner," she said.

"Sure thing," Jonas said, then gestured to Goliath. "When you're ready to sell him, name your price."

"There's not enough money for that," Connie said. She watched as he opened a beer, handed it to Harry, and joined him on the sofa.

"It'll never happen," Harry concurred. "She loves him like a kid."

"C'mon, it's a win-win." Jonas reasoned. "You'll get breeding rights,"

"I don't want to hear about selling my dogs," she said.

Harry took a sip of beer and ran a hand through his hair. "Especially Goliath," he added.

"Just think about it," Jonas said.

"There's nothing to think about," Connie stated. She reached for her purse and kissed Harry on the cheek. "See you in the morning."

He reached for her hand and pressed it to his cheek. "See you, dear."

"Don't forget to give the pups their pills. I set them out," Connie reminded, then turned to Jonas. "Goodbye," she said.

When Connie arrived home the following morning, two pups fought over a toy in the kitchen. Magnolia and another bully stood beside empty food dishes.

"No one's fed you yet?" she asked. Harry sprawled on the sofa with the TV on. She walked over and touched his shoulder. "You forgot to feed the dogs."

He moaned, touched his forehead, and turned his head to reveal bruising and swelling on the left side of his face.

"What happened?" Connie asked. She kneeled before him and gently helped him sit up. "We better get you to the hospital."

"Can't go," he mumbled. "Jonas."

"Let's get ice on that." She pressed a hand to his cheek. "Jonas did this?"

"They took him." Harry lowered his head.

"Took who?" Connie asked and guided him to a chair at the kitchen table. A partial bottle of whiskey sat on the counter. She scanned the room for all her dogs. "Where's Goliath?"

Harry held out a crumpled check.

"You sold Goliath?"

"Jonas made a heck of an offer," he said. "We get breeding rights. He was supposed to take him in a few weeks so you could get used to the idea." He traced a finger over his swollen cheek. "Then his son showed up. I tried to stop them."

"No," she cried and stood with palms flat on the table.

Harry reached for her, but she smacked his hand away. He slumped in this chair and stared as she shredded the check and dropped it in the middle of the table. She went to the freezer, threw a pack of peas before him, and made a pot of coffee.

Magnolia nuzzled her pant leg, prompting Connie to wash the dog bowls and put out their food. One of the puppies slopped water from one of the bowls, creating a mucky mess. Connie picked him up and mopped the area dry.

When the coffee pot gurgled completion, she poured

two cups and sat across from Harry. She tapped her finger on the mug and then raised it to her lips. Her hand trembled. "You sold my boy?" she said.

"I made a big mistake." Harry lowered his head. "I'll tell Jonas the deal is off."

"You broke my heart, Harry Donaldson," Connie whispered. "You know he's my boy. Ours."

He nodded. "I'm sorry, hon. I was wrong. I'll get him back."

"It's not about money. We have each other and the dogs," Connie whispered. "You'll never get our dog back from that lowlife."

"You lost Billy and Goliath," Maryah whispered.

"I haven't talked about them in ages." Connie dabbed a tear away. "Loving can break your heart, but it's also the greatest healer."

Maryah shook her head. There it was. "You're telling me I have some healing to do?" she asked.

"Honey, you're sitting where Harry and I sat years ago that morning. Some things we never forget, but don't let the past hold you prisoner." Connie reached for a cigarette.

"You don't beat around the bush." Maryah gave a small smile and tried for a cheerful tone.

"I never threw it in Harry's face, but things were never the same between us," Connie said. "His drinking escalated. He wasn't a mean drunk, just a feel-sorry-for-yourself type."

"When I was drinking, sometimes I was a jerk before I

passed out," Maryah admitted. "I supposed I ought to talk to Lars about it."

"It helps to clear the air," Connie said softly. "How about a cup of coffee, and we get pizza?"

"Sounds good," Maryah said, glancing at her watch—almost six o'clock. Time flew during her visits with Connie. "I'll text Lars and let him know I'll be home later," she said, reaching for her phone.

The dogs came over, and one nuzzled Connie's hand. Another hopped up on the sofa beside her recliner. "I think they're telling me it's their suppertime," she said.

"Another reason why MayBea adores you." Maryah laughed. "Lars says your dogs eat better than he does."

"Donaldson dogs are spoiled for certain. My dogs get chicken and kibble." Connie scooped up a puppy and set it before her on the table.

"I'll feed them," Maryah offered. She went over to the fridge, knowing the routine well.

"You got it, kid. I never refuse help." Connie grinned.

Maryah placed a casserole dish on the counter.

## ✤ 4 ✤

That evening, Maryah drove back from Connie's, thinking over what her friend had shared about losing two beloved pets in such a dramatic way. Connie's words played through her mind, "we all have our baggage." True enough, but Connie didn't have *her* baggage.

She pulled into the grocery store parking lot. Lars had asked her to pick up a few items on the way home. She slowed as she drove by Liquor Land. A glass of red wine would do nicely. Just one glass. Just one.

Lars would probably bitch, but if she'd drink it out of a mug, he might not notice. Maryah pulled into a parking spot and hopped from the car. Although it was a cool evening, she opened all the windows a few inches before locking the vehicle.

MayBea shifted in her dog carrier in the back seat.

"I'll be back in a few," she called over her shoulder. The intense visit with Connie and almost losing MayBea weighed on her. The stress of it all, yes, she could have just one glass of wine.

Later that evening, at home in her recliner, Maryah dozed off after finishing a bottle of wine.

~

MayBea's ears twitched as she struggled to sit up. She leaned against the sofa where Maryah snored and pushed against her leg.

Maryah sprawled on the cushions. A mug was knocked over on the end table, and an empty wineglass sat beside it.

MayBea eyed it. Whenever Maryah drank it, she and Lars "had words." This time he walked out, leaving MayBea to keep vigil. He'd never left them, despite many fights when Maryah would yell.

"Humans are not like us," Goliath had told her. "They can be cruelest to those closest to them."

This morning MayBea's body ached, the agony reaching a new level. Lars wasn't there to give her the pill that eased the discomfort. When would he return? They needed him.

Goliath had given in to her pleas for more time with her people. The increasing gulf between them saddened her.

MayBea grunted and bumped against Maryah's leg. "Wake up."

The dawn let scant light into the room, providing enough illumination to reveal Goliath opposite her. It was unusual she had not sensed him.

"Uhh, uhhmm," MayBea greeted him. How long had he been present? "Stay. I need to stay with her. She will need me most today."

Goliath gave an almost imperceptible nod. MayBea did not know how much time she had. She applied more pressure against Maryah. Time was running out.

Ouch. Maryah's head pounded as she opened her eyes. Where the hell was she? The sofa creaked as she rolled over. She'd slept in her clothes—again. She pulled the quilt about her against the chill of the November morning. Autumn meant cooler weather, even in Southern California.

She groaned and had vague memories of the night before. Stomach cramps warned that food might not be a good idea. Last night she downed a bottle of wine in record time, then discovered the tequila behind the flour canister in the cupboard. Lars liked the occasional margarita. Hard liquor wasn't her friend. Damn, why the hell couldn't she have left it alone? If only she'd stuck with the wine.

Maryah stretched. Her neck and back ached. Lars leaving her on the sofa indicated that all would not be cozy and content on the home front. She fumbled for her cell phone to see if she'd called or texted anyone, hoping damage control wasn't necessary.

She'd shower, grab a coffee, stomach pills, and aspirin. Ugh, only 6 a.m. She propped herself up and groaned. A wave of dizziness hit her like bed spins. She raised a hand to her temple.

Her text messages showed one from Lars.

*Lars: You were out of control. Can't take it anymore. I'm at Connie's.*

Maryah stared at the text and reread it. Shit. Connie would know she'd fallen off the wagon. Her face felt warm. Shame and guilt weren't new to her. But damn, only yesterday, Connie had been telling her how proud she was of her. This, after she'd given her the "you better straighten up, or you're going to lose him" talk.

Maryah felt the feathery sandpaper sensation of MayBea licking her leg. At least her dog hadn't deserted her.

She leaned back against the sofa. Crap. She hung her head. It was true. She couldn't have just one and drink like other people. She'd get to a meeting as soon as her headache and dizziness allowed and admit she had relapsed.

The ringing of her phone clamored for attention. Who the hell would be calling so early on a Saturday? Puzzled that it was her older brother calling, she pressed the answer button. Even though he was on the East Coast, Tommy never called this early. Had Lars reached out to Tommy to give her a lecture?

She rolled her eyes and tried to sound nonchalant when she picked up.

"Hey, Tommy," she said. "What's up?"

At first, Tommy said nothing, but breathed hard. "He's gone," he sobbed.

Lars must've given him an earful for Tommy to be distressed. "He'll be back," she replied.

"No, he's gone," Tommy repeated.

Maryah shook her head. "Lars is at Connie's," she said. "He'll be back."

"No, it's Danny," Tommy said.

Danny? Their brother? "What about Danny?" she asked.

"He's gone," Tommy said.

Not her Danny. Tommy had named his son after their brother. "You mean your son?" she amended. "Is he OK?" Shit. No. No. No.

"Our brother, Danny," Tommy wept. "He died last night."

Maryah trembled. Not true. A lie. "Not Danny," she cried. "Our little brother? This isn't supposed to happen." Her insides heaved, and she felt the air knocked from her. She screamed and fell to her knees. "How?" she choked out.

"He had a heart attack at a baseball game last night. Died at the hospital," Tommy responded. "Lisa and Candace were with him."

"It's not true," she sobbed. "I don't believe you."

When her little brother had been dying three thousand miles away in Virginia, she'd been a shit-ass drunk passed out on the sofa, obnoxious enough for her husband to leave.

She dropped the phone and curled up on the carpet. MayBea moved beside her and nuzzled her arm. Maryah pulled the dog to her and began to weep. "It should've been me," she cried. "Melody, I did it again. It should've been me."

Maryah sat on the floor, back against the sofa. MayBea sat with her head propped against her shoulder. Numb and exhausted from weeping, Maryah wiped away her tears.

Memories assaulted her senses of the last time she saw Danny, the text messages and photos he'd sent her a few days earlier. Then her thoughts drifted to thirty years earlier, when they'd lost Melody.

She didn't know how much time had passed since Tommy's call. She sat numb, wondering what to do next. She needed Lars. As if on cue, the back door opened.

"I'm glad you're home," she called, her voice trembling. "Did Tommy call you?"

"No."

Maryah's heart skipped a beat. Footsteps sounded behind her. She turned to kneel, propping her arms on the sofa to push herself up on unsteady legs.

Her brother stood in his typical garb, sports team T-shirt, shorts, and sneakers. Danny stood near the window with the sunlight streaming around him, giving him an ethereal appearance.

She felt the blood drain from her face. "Is this a dream?" asked Maryah.

"I wish it were," he said. "I died last night."

The blood pounded in her ears. She moved to lean against the fireplace for support. She was hallucinating, imagining it all. "This must be a dream," Maryah rasped.

"I'm not a dream." Danny sounded exasperated.

"What happened?" she whispered.

"I was at a ball game with Lisa and Candace," he said. "I went to the concession stand. When I was in line, I got a strange pain in my chest and went to sit down."

She covered her mouth with a hand to stifle a cry.

Danny ran a hand through his light brown hair, the same color as hers. "The next thing I know, my wife and daughter were standing over me, grief-stricken, and I couldn't do anything to help them."

A sharp pain kicked at her gut. Maryah clenched both hands across her stomach and closed her eyes. When she opened them, her brother was still there. "Are you an angel? My angel?"

"You could say that, " Danny answered.

"The last text you sent me included a selfie of you and Candace. You looked fine. What did I miss?" she pressed. "How could I not have known you were at risk of a heart attack just like Daddy?"

Danny sighed. "Don't do what you always do."

He sounded a bit testy for an angel, like when they got into one of their sibling squabbles.

"What does that mean?" she asked, trying to keep the edge from her tone.

"You make my dying about you." He responded with his usual directness. "Because you feel guilty."

"Guilt," Maryah snapped. "Why would I feel guilty?"

In his typical way, he rolled his eyes, irritating her even more. "Yeah, right."

"But you're too young to go," Maryah chastised.

"Ah, still the same bossy sister," he sighed. "As if I had any control over any of this."

Their banter made it seem normal between them. She could tell it wasn't true.

"No, sis," Danny replied. "It's true."

The back door clicked open, and keys jangled against the counter.

Danny gestured toward the kitchen. "Time for me to go."

"Tommy called," Lars announced as he walked into the room, his expression grim.

Maryah gazed at him, then back to where her brother had stood.

"Danny's gone," she whispered. Her cheeks felt warm, and the room began to spin.

Lars nodded.

"It's not true," Maryah whimpered before passing out.

# 5

MayBea licked Maryah's face. "Uhh, uhhmm." She snorted. "Help her."

Lars kneeled beside Maryah and touched her cheek. "Honey," he said, and put a hand on her shoulder.

MayBea recalled the ache when her littermate, Hercules, left. She still missed him. The pain filled her. It must be the same for Maryah. "Uhh, uhhmm." MayBea nuzzled Lars. "We need you."

"Oh," Maryah moaned.

"Are you OK?" Lars asked and helped her to sit up.

"I'm glad you came back," she whispered, caressing his cheek. "I'm sorry."

"Tommy called me. It's a shock for us both. Let's get you up," he soothed.

Goliath sat underneath the window with morning light filling the room. But it was the appearance of Brother-Angel that drew her attention.

MayBea followed Lars and pressed her against him. Her people needed her. How on earth could she leave them? She watched Goliath and followed his gaze to where Brother-Angel hovered. Neither Lars nor Maryah appeared to see him.

What did it mean that Brother-Angel stayed close?

Goliath raised his head and gazed at her, a warning not to intrude. In his alive days in the world, he'd been the finest English Bulldog from their breeder-lady, Connie.

MayBea never questioned him, for he was her ancestor and mentor. Instinct told her that he also had unfinished business in the human world. Perhaps as long as he did, she could remain to watch over Maryah.

Brother-Angel lingered near where Maryah moaned.

"You're remembering, sis?" Brother-Angel asked. "It's OK. I'm here for you."

It was evident to MayBea that her owners could not hear his words.

Lars guided Maryah to the sofa and sat beside her. He wrapped an arm around her, rubbing her shoulder. MayBea climbed up to sit on the other side and leaned her chin against Maryah's shoulder.

"Uhh uhhmm." MayBea tried to tell her. "He came back to us."

Maryah leaned against Lars and began to weep. "Danny was here."

"It's the shock," Lars said and hugged her.

"It's OK, sis." Brother-Angel kneeled in front of her.

MayBea tilted her head and watched him. She liked him for the way he tried to comfort Maryah.

"I saw Danny. I saw him," Maryah repeated.

Lars covered her hand with his. "Look, it's been a rough twenty-four hours."

"You can say that again," Brother-Angel said.

The next day, Maryah and Lars sat in the kitchen, laptop open in front of them. They were trying to arrange for travel to Virginia for Danny's memorial service.

Maryah shook her head. In the space of a few hours, her world had changed. Had she been hallucinating when she saw her brother?

MayBea sat on her doggie bed, watching them.

"It's like MayBea knows we've lost my brother," she whispered.

Lars glanced up. "She's a special dog."

Maryah glanced at him. How like her dear husband to avoid talking about her drunken debacle and help her pick up the pieces. He hadn't mentioned her relapse and ensuing behavior. Instead, he'd taken care of her, stayed by her side, and treated her like the wife he deserved, not the wife she was.

Allowing her to get away with crap didn't bode well for her. Danny would've called her on it. That's why she'd bicker with her brother sometimes in their sibling fashion. He called her on her crap.

"I don't remember your leaving that night," Maryah stated. There. She'd called attention to the pink elephant in the room. "What did you tell Connie?"

Lars looked uncomfortable. "We don't have to do this now."

"My heart's broken," she covered his hand with hers and choked back a sob. "I need to talk about my behavior and not let it get swept under the rug because of losing my brother. It's easy for me to hide behind that."

He nodded. "How long have you been drinking?"

"That night was the first time in ages," she admitted.

"Why?" he asked, sliding his chair back from the table. "Everything was going so well."

"I don't know," she shrugged and looked away. "I'd dreamed about Melody, and it all came back."

"Melody's been gone for thirty years," he said.

She shook her head, knowing he would never understand. "Why did you leave?" she asked, forcing the topic they both evaded so well.

"You don't remember?" Lars stood up and retrieved the coffeepot to refill his cup.

"Was I a jerk?" Maryah persisted. She needed to know.

"You were crying that it was your fault Melody died," Lars said. "I tried to hug you. You started cussing and pushed me away. That was the beginning."

Maryah's heart thumped. "Worse than a jerk," she stated.

"Much worse," Lars said.

"I'm sorry. I want to quit," Maryah said and went to where he sat. She hugged him, half expecting him to push her away. "I don't deserve you."

"You kept cussing at me, following me into the bedroom," he replied. "I figured the best thing to do was leave. I got in the car and started driving, then called Connie. I didn't know what else to do."

"You did the right thing. I'm sorry you had to go through that," Maryah said. "It was right to call Connie."

"She told me to come over and let you sleep it off." Lars held her. "Then Tommy called about Danny. He was worried about you."

"You're the best." She wrapped her arms around him. "I love you." Her voice broke.

He wrapped an arm around her waist and guided her to the table.

"Connie said her husband relapsed a few times." Lars studied her. "She's coming by later."

"Ironic isn't it, that the night my little brother died, I was drunk and crying about losing my baby sister," she pondered.

"Kind of weird," Lars agreed.

A wave of the stark reality of Danny's sudden death washed over her. Despite the sunlight filling their San Diego kitchen, Maryah shivered. "Danny died from a heart attack, just like our father. He was too young." She lowered her head and whimpered. "I should've known he was at risk."

Maryah had been studying her cell phone messages from Danny. She'd scrutinized photos and texts for the hundredth time, searching for a sign of ill health behind his enthusiastic demeanor.

"What could I have missed?" she asked.

"How could you have known?" Lars responded.

"Genetics. Our father and two uncles passed away from a massive heart attack," Maryah explained. "Danny was at risk, and I missed it."

"It's not your fault." Lars sat in the recliner.

Maryah looked down. A fresh bout of tears came over her. The pain was almost unbearable.

"We always think we could've done more," Lars said.

She kneeled beside him and intertwined her fingers with his. "I'm sorry," she whispered, feeling like she'd been kicked in the gut. "Yet you stayed with me."

"You still don't know why?" Lars asked.

Maryah swallowed hard and wiped tears away with the back of her hand. "No," she said in a hoarse voice.

"It comes down to the same thing. What you think you don't deserve, and why I stay." He stroked her cheek. "Love."

Maryah buried her head in his chest; heaving sobs racked her. She wept for Danny, Lars, and herself.

Sometime later, she sat beside him on the sofa. "We never talk." She sighed.

"Yeah, I'm not big on a lot of flowery chatter," he confirmed, his arm around her.

"I'm glad you stuck by me," she murmured.

"You give up too easily." He shifted on the sofa.

MayBea walked over and stared at them until Lars helped her to the sofa. She curled up between them.

"Dan led you to me," he stated.

"True. It was love at first sight," she said. Despite her anguish, she smiled at the memory of their first meeting.

"I knew Dan had a sister, but never saw you until that night."

It'd been the night of Danny and Lisa's engagement party. Maryah thought she'd met all of his friends until she spotted Lars.

"That moment changed my life," she declared. She'd been smitten by his perfect smile and sense of humor. Oh, her heart fluttered the first time she saw him.

Connie pulled into the driveway, precluding further discussion. MayBea got down from the sofa and followed Lars out to greet her.

Maryah joined them, watching as MayBea melted into Connie's arms. "Once a Donaldson dog, always," Connie declared.

"So true," Maryah agreed. "She knew it was you when you pulled up."

Connie wrapped her in a hug. The sweet, familiar comfort of her friend brought on more tears.

"I'm sorry," Maryah rasped.

"C'mon, dear, let's sit," Connie suggested.

Maryah nodded and gestured to the teakettle. "OK, I'll make you a cup."

Lars touched her shoulder. "I'll do it."

Maryah sat on the sofa and helped MayBea up. The dog positioned herself so that her chin rested on Maryah's knee.

Connie sat in one of the recliners facing her. "I'm sorry about your brother, dear," she said.

"Thank you." Maryah blinked back another onslaught of tears. "I told Lars I think Danny inherited the heart problems, and I got the one with alcohol."

"That might be true," Connie stated in her matter-of-fact way.

"Are you going to ask why I got drunk?" Maryah asked.

"I was married to an alcoholic," Connie said, giving her a knowing look. "You probably don't know yourself."

Maryah nodded. "I'm going to a meeting later and will admit what happened."

"I imagine it's not easy," Connie said.

"It's what I have to do," Maryah swallowed. The humiliation of walking back into a meeting paled compared to what she'd put her husband through.

Lars placed a cup of tea in front of them, then sat on the other side of MayBea on the sofa. "She thinks it's her fault her brother died," he said.

"I failed them both," Maryah said, trying to keep her voice from shaking.

"You don't have a crystal ball," Connie reasoned.

"Melody fell through the ice. Dan died from a heart attack," Lars said.

"I never should've let Melody try my skates," Maryah stated. "Knowing our family genetics, I should've warned Danny."

"Melody might've gone anyway. Kids don't listen," Lars said. "As for Dan, how do you know they would've detected anything preventable?"

Maryah reached for a tissue.

"You can spend a lifetime questioning what-ifs," Lars said. "It's also an excuse to keep from going on."

Connie studied them, then pointed to Lars. "This one's a keeper. When he speaks, it's because he has something to say."

Maryah reached for his hand. "Sometimes I forget that." She mulled over Connie's advice. "He's put up with a lot of my melodrama."

Lars shifted under the attention. He could be a rock, but didn't like to be at the center of attention.

"Harry and I never spoke about Goliath after it happened," Connie revealed.

Maryah nodded and hugged a pillow to her.

"After we got him back, I realized that guilt ate away at Harry all those years," she said. "By not talking about it, the remorse and anger built up. Goliath's coming home healed the wound, but the pain and scar lingered."

"The past and present, sometimes they're too closely intertwined." Maryah scratched MayBea on the head.

"Why can't I be more like her?" She gestured to the dog. "She doesn't keep score. It's unconditional love."

"Then stop keeping score," Connie advised. "Let it go."

"I'll try," she said. It was Danny who'd once told her that she tended to hold grudges. It had made her angry. He stood his ground, telling her she was mad because he was right.

"When you get back, maybe you should see a grief counselor," Connie suggested. "My friend said it helped her."

Maryah glanced at Lars. "You think I should?"

"With everything you've been through, it's not a bad idea," he said.

Maryah tilted her head back, realizing the idea had merit. "My old way of coping wasn't so good."

"It will help," Connie encouraged.

Maryah slowly nodded. Despite the ache in her heart, she felt deep gratitude for her husband and dear friend.

"Can you tell me one thing?" she asked.

"What's that?" Connie responded.

"I want to know how you got Goliath back," Maryah said.

# ☙ 6 ❧

After a few years, Donaldson's Bulldogs flourished again. Harry left raising the dogs to Connie. She became an anchor in bulldog rescue.

On an autumn Sunday afternoon, she received a call from an old-time bulldogger, Jim McDougal. He had a dog he'd picked up from a shelter. Jim lived about an hour away.

"He's eight or nine years old, got mange, had a bad case of fleas, and is a bit underweight," Jim said. "But you can see he's a fine bully."

Connie glanced at Harry dozing on the sofa and two dogs on either side of him. "We can get him tomorrow," she said.

"Can you come today?" Jim asked. "You need to see him."

Connie reached for a cigarette and tapped it on the counter, but didn't light it. "What does he look like?" she asked.

"You need to see this dog," Jim repeated. "He's fawn-colored, a white patch over one eye, and one white paw.

"Which paw is white?"

"The right front," Jim said.

She fell to her knees. "It can't be."

"Get here when you can," Jim urged. "We'll be waiting."

Her dogs surrounded her, thinking she wanted to play a game. One of the puppies squeezed a chew toy that squeaked, waking Harry up. She hugged her dogs, then struggled to her feet, wiping away tears.

Harry muted the TV and sat up. "Everything OK, dear?" he asked.

Connie straightened, strode over to him, and extended a hand. "We have a rescue to pick up," she said.

Neither Connie nor Harry spoke on the drive to Jim's for several minutes. His hand trembled as he fumbled with the radio buttons. She pulled the van off the interstate at an exit and parked on the roadside. She undid her seat belt and turned to him.

Harry hung his head. "I'm sorry," he cried.

"I forgave you long ago. If I never told you, then *I'm* sorry." Her voice caught, then she hugged him. "If this isn't our Goliath, we go on. I love you. Let's make this right."

"Yes, my dear. Let's bring our boy home." He managed a smile.

For a moment, it was the old Harry. Connie pulled back onto the interstate, and the rest of the drive went by in a blur.

Jim was seated on the front porch when they pulled into his ten-acre ranch. He had lived alone since the death of his wife a few years earlier, but for his dogs and a few farm animals. Connie had bred one of her finer litters to his sire, Champion McDougal's Mighty Mac.

Three of his dogs came up, scurrying at her feet. She greeted each by name, following them to the porch.

Jim stood and shook hands with Harry. He leaned over and hugged her, then gestured toward the screen door. "He's in the back bedroom. I put a kiddie gate up to keep the others from pestering him. Handsome dog. You can see he's been through a bit."

Connie placed a hand on her chest and waited for him.

"You go on back. I'll be here," Jim said, then sat down.

Harry sat down beside him. "Looks like we'll be getting more rain," he said.

"We might, but the worst of the storm's already passed," Jim responded.

Connie opened the door, ensuring the other dogs didn't trail after her. She walked down a hallway, following a rasping bulldog snore.

She stood at the kiddie gate, watching the sleeping dog. It took her three tries before she could whistle without crying. Then she began a clear whistling of "Mary Had a Little Lamb." Over the years, anytime she saw one of her dogs, they'd come to her upon hearing the tune.

An underweight fawn-colored bulldog continued to snore. His right front paw was white. Connie whistled louder. The dog's ears twitched, his eyes opened, then he raised his head.

Connie stepped over the kiddie gate and dropped to one knee.

He limped over, leaned against her, and pressed his head against her in his familiar way.

She stopped whistling and began to cry. She ran her hands over the lean form, trembling when he winced in pain. The scars and anomalies bespoke his past. Goliath leaned against her and licked her face, wiping away the tears. She held him in a feather-soft hug.

"Harry Donaldson, c'mon back here," she called after finding her voice. "It's our boy. Our handsome boy is home."

Later, she stood with Jim when Harry carried Goliath to the van. "How did you find him?" she asked.

"Several of us have had our eyes out for years," Jim answered. "I thought it might be him, but didn't want to get your hopes up."

She reached out and touched his leathery cheek. "Thank you from the bottom of my heart."

Jim hooked his thumbs in his belt loops and gazed at her. "Jonas will never breed another bully again or own one."

Connie blinked and then exhaled. "I never thought this day would come. My poor boy. How can I make it up to him?"

"Dogs aren't like us, Connie, especially the bullies," he stated. "They don't keep a scorecard of what we've done, holding us prisoner for our mistakes. Take your cue from Goliath and make the most of your time with them."

# 7

The next day Maryah and Lars sat in the terminal watching planes taxi while they waited to board a flight to Richmond. A chill ran through her, and she pulled her coat tighter around her.

The wall-mounted televisions in the bar across the way played ball games and talk shows. Still just before noon, but people lined up at the bar with drinks of beer, wine, and her most forbidden item—whiskey on the rocks. How inviting it looked. It was a happy hour for these travelers from various places. Not for her.

It had been four days since her relapse and when Tommy had called to tell her about Danny. Still incomprehensible. What would it be like to be a "normie," as her friends in recovery called folks who could have an occasional drink?

The bartender poured a glass of wine for two women at the mahogany bar. One of them held a cigarette. Oh yes, that beckoned to her too. The old ways, the old days, back before she'd met her Lars.

On occasion, she'd given in to temptation and had a cigarette at Connie's. Smoking had been something she could take or leave. But not the booze. Lars had been her salvation. He never smoked and hated to be around it. He drank like a gentleman, never getting drunk. It did not affect him as it did her.

The old anxiousness and desire ran through her like a current. That's what she wanted, to be at the bar, cigarette in one hand and wineglass in the other, transported from the pain.

Lars leaned against her and smoothed her hair. "What are you thinking?"

"Honestly?" she asked.

"Yes," he responded.

"What I hate most about being sober is that you have to 'feel the feelings,' as they say," she replied. "It sucks and makes me realize how I used alcohol to numb the pain so I wouldn't have to deal with things."

His eyes grew wide. "Wow," he said.

"Yeah, it's all kind of weird." Maryah sighed.

"That's why it will probably help for you to talk to the grief counselor when we get back," he suggested. "You're still crying over Mellie, and that's been thirty years."

Maryah's heart began to pound, and her palms felt sweaty. What he didn't know. "Between Mellie and Danny, I feel responsible," she replied and yawned. Sleep had been elusive for the past few days. Hopefully, she could get a decent snooze in on the plane.

The ticket agent announced boarding for their flight. Lars held out a hand and helped her up to get in line. A nap would be most welcome.

Maryah closed her eyes and leaned back in her seat while the plane taxied for takeoff. She leaned back against the headrest. Lars pulled her seat belt tighter around her and patted her hand.

The whir of the engines became the sound of waves in Maryah's dream. She stood on a beach she'd never been to before. In the distance, she saw what looked like Danny walking away.

Maryah ran after him. "Danny?" she called.

He stopped and turned. It wasn't Danny.

"Daddy?" she cried.

It was her father, gone for over twenty years. Taller than she remembered and somehow different. Joe Giancano had worked construction, and in the summer, due to his Italian heritage, his skin became a glorious deeper reddish brown. He wore khakis, work boots, and a work shirt.

"Dad?" Maryah repeated.

He shook his head. Maryah could see it wasn't her father, so close yet not.

"I'm Giuseppe," he said. "Each person has a guardian angel," he explained. "We're assigned to you from birth until we bring you Home. Danny conceptualized me as the image of your father. He called me Giuseppe."

"You're his guardian angel?" she whispered. Part of their Irish-Italian upbringing was they believed each individual had a special angel, and you could name them.

"Yes, Danny Boy is why I am here," Giuseppe confirmed, using one of her favorite nicknames for her brother. "Do you know who your guardian angel is?"

"Yes, I do," Maryah replied. Shouldn't *he* know that? "I call him Antonio."

"Antonio's one of our best," Giuseppe said. "He's had his hands full with you."

Maryah chose to ignore the barb. Weren't angels supposed to be benevolent? So far, Giuseppe was missing the mark.

"My brother still had a lot of living left to do and none of the risk factors for heart disease." She tried to keep the edge from her voice. "I think he was taken too soon."

The tide was coming in, forcing them further up the beach, empty but for themselves. Maryah struggled to keep up with him.

"In this, you are correct." Giuseppe gave a slight nod. His intense gaze made her uncomfortable. "There is much to be sorted out."

"Sort what out?" Maryah asked. As much as Giuseppe looked like her father, he was nothing like Joe Giancano. Her father had been congenial, sweet, and funny. Giuseppe's dark glare and somber manner were unnerving. "Why did I see Danny? Is he my angel too?"

"Call it a special assignment. He is here to help you," Giuseppe replied.

"Special assignment? It seems you need help more than I do," she said.

Giuseppe shook a finger at her. "Ah, Antonio said you are stubborn, angry, and defiant."

Maryah frowned and mimicked his gesture. She wasn't that bad. "What about you? I'd say disagreeable, bossy, and unreasonable. Nothing like Danny or my father."

"You are not so bad, but perhaps not so good. You have much to learn." Giuseppe took a step forward, giving her a stern look. "Antonio does not have an easy subject."

She resisted the urge to take a step back. "So, I'm not a saint." She placed her hands on her hips. "I'm only human."

"Yes, most lucky that you still are," he said. The wind picked up. The waves hit harder against the rocks with a roar.

"I don't understand," she said. "What does this have to do with Danny?"

Giuseppe exhaled. "An angel is often joyful when he can bring his subject Home. Antonio was troubled when he saw *you*r name on the Return Calendar. Your family wanted to know why. He broke a sacred rule and told them."

"What are you talking about?" Maryah whispered. Her stomach dropped. A feeling akin to dread began to creep through her.

"Antonio wanted to give you more time," he lowered his voice. "Danny Boy paid the price for that choice. He was more ready than you."

She felt like she'd been sucker punched in the gut. She fell to her knees. "Danny was taken instead of me?" she gasped.

Giuseppe folded his arms and nodded. "Yes," he said. "Most unusual."

"Get him back," Maryah begged.

"It cannot be amended," Giuseppe sounded weary.

"Oh, my goodness. What can I do?" Maryah raised her gaze to his. The sun cast a few rays streaming across the horizon over Giuseppe. His silhouette showed the outline of wings she hadn't seen before. "Please help me."

There was a shift in his demeanor. He kneeled beside her, his wings shielding them from the wind. Giuseppe tilted his head and touched her shoulder.

"Start with forgiveness. The rest shall come," he said in a gentle voice.

# 8

A few hours later, Maryah and Lars arrived in Richmond. She let him guide her off the plane. She pulled her coat about her. The late November evening was far colder here than it had been in Southern California.

Lars gave her a worried look and reached for her hand. "We'll get through this," he promised.

Maryah nodded and chose to keep the dream about Giuseppe to herself. She'd need more than a grief counselor to help her. Dreams, hallucinations? Had her world gone topsy-turvy over losing her brother, and she was hanging on by a thread?

Her oldest brother, Tommy, met them at baggage claim. He wore a Red Sox baseball cap, just like her father and Danny always had. Growing up in Massachusetts, the Giancanos had adored the Red Sox with New England fervor. The resemblance between her brothers, both tall with blue eyes, brought on another fresh wave of tears.

"We're the only ones left," she cried.

After a few hours at their hotel, they headed to the funeral parlor.

Inside, several monitors displayed a montage of photos of her brother in special moments with family and friends. It showed the real Danny Boy, her nickname for him, his true self. It was lovely and broke her heart.

She stood silent, dumbfounded, and grateful, watching the rolling display of her brother's life. An urn sat next to a large photo of him. Danny Boy had been cremated.

After some time, Maryah entered an empty sitting room, leaving the door cracked. Out of sight, she collapsed into a chair and reached for a tissue. Her head throbbed.

Maryah lowered her head to her hands and began to weep. "What have I done?"

"Why do you always blame yourself?" he asked.

Maryah sat speechless at seeing him. Danny was at the funeral home. At his wake. It wasn't real. It must be a breakdown. Until now, she believed it was a dream or due to lack of sleep.

"No, you're not having a breakdown," Danny replied. He wore the same Washington Senators minor league baseball team T-shirt he had the last time she saw him. This time he wore a Red Sox hat.

"This is what I was wearing when I passed," he said. "It's the hat you sent me for my birthday last year. I'm not a dream."

"I'm delusional, or you're a ghost." She struggled to keep the panic from her voice.

"You always overthink everything." He shrugged.

Maryah rose to stand in front of him. "Is this how you looked right before?" He was a good-size guy. Heavier than the last time she had seen him.

Danny crossed his arms. "Yep, pretty much." He did little to conceal his irritation over her inspection.

She marveled that as a ghost, angel, or whatever, he could be cantankerous. But that was who they were together.

"Like you were Miss Congeniality?" He taunted in their sibling fashion.

Their old rapport comforted her, although his newfound ability to understand some of her thoughts unnerved her.

"If I had taken the time to visit you," she admitted after finishing her perusal, "I might've seen it coming."

Danny shook his head. "I don't think anyone saw this coming."

"There's something I have to tell you," Maryah began. Her heart began to pound.

A knock sounded on the door.

Danny flashed a smile. "We'll have to take this up later."

"Come in," Maryah called.

Lars entered and looked around. "I thought I heard you talking to someone." He lowered himself to the chair beside her, dark circles under his eyes.

"Just talking to myself." She rasped and stifled a sob. "How are you holding up?"

"OK." He leaned back in the chair.

A tap on the semi-open door sounded. A gentleman in a suit stepped inside. He wore a name tag, Lou, Funeral Director.

"Can I get you anything? Coffee, water?" Lou offered.

"Coffee would be great," Maryah answered.

"Same for me," Lars said, and stood. "I'll get it if you show me where it is."

"Thank you," Maryah said, waiting for the door to close. "Danny?" she called.

She had to tell him the truth. Bile rose in her throat, a sour, acidic taste. If only it were a horrid dream that Danny had passed. But Giuseppe's message made it more like a psychotic episode.

She lowered her head to her hands.

"I'm here, sis," he said. He sat across from her, looking every bit alive and vibrant.

"Do you know what I'm thinking?" she wondered.

"Not always," he said.

"I had a dream. I saw Giuseppe," she said quietly.

"Giuseppe?" he asked. "My angel?"

"He said you were taken prematurely," she whispered. The blood pounded in her ears, and her face felt hot. She held her breath.

Danny stared for a long moment before speaking. He leaned forward, elbows on his knees. "Why would he tell you that?" he sounded dubious.

She took a deep breath, her heart pounding. The words stuck in her throat. "Because of me, little brother," she said at last. Tears streamed down her cheeks. "It was supposed to have been me."

"You instead of me?" Danny rose and began to pace the

length of the room. He made two passes back and forth before she answered.

"Giuseppe said I wasn't ready and needed more time," Maryah uttered. She lowered her head. She sounded pathetic and ludicrous even to herself.

He stopped pacing and faced the wall, his back to her. "What about me? Didn't I need more time with my wife and daughter?" he bellowed. "What's next? I complete my assignment and return from this limbo?"

Maryah shook her head. "No. Giuseppe said you can't come back." She felt sick to her stomach. Maryah stood on shaky legs and moved beside him. She didn't dare touch him. "I'm sorry."

He placed his palms against the wall and gave her a sideways glance. "Sorry won't get me back to my wife and daughter and make up for everything I'll miss in their lives," Danny whispered, and looked down.

A knock on the door sounded, and in an instant, Danny was gone. She opened it to Lars, who held two cups of coffee.

"Hope you like it black," he said.

Maryah accepted a cup and sank onto the loveseat. She fell back against the pillows, closed her eyes, and sipped the coffee. It must've been sitting for ages. But although bitter and lukewarm, she savored it.

Lars touched her cheek, studying her. "Hey, are you OK?"

She covered her hand with his. "You're always here for me, strong and steady when I screw up." A small sob escaped her. "I need you, Lars. Always have."

He touched her hair. "I'm glad you remembered."

~

They re-entered the central area of the funeral home and joined Tommy in a makeshift receiving line for folks offering condolences. Many people came to pay their respects. Danny had many friends drawn to him by his charisma and good nature.

Maryah tired and sat before a monitor that scrolled a photo montage of Danny's life. There were photos of his wedding, holding Candace when she was born, coaching her in softball, and with numerous friends.

She watched as the display showed childhood photos of the four siblings. As the youngest, Mellie was always in the front center, then Tommy, Danny, and herself. The grief welled up in her, and she let the tears flow.

At the hotel that night, Maryah spoke little, overwhelmed by the surreal events of the day. She crawled into bed, still trying to figure out how to get Danny back.

Lars fell asleep, and Maryah lay in bed awake. She glanced at the clock, only 10 p.m. The bathroom light provided enough illumination to dress and find her purse and room key. She headed to the lobby, hoping to stretch her legs and get some air.

The hotel restaurant was closed, but she could see a few folks, most likely business travelers, at the bar. Maryah walked in, maybe just a diet coke or a rum and coke to help her sleep.

She climbed onto the barstool and glanced at the game on the television. The bartender nodded and placed a cocktail napkin in front of her.

"What will it be?" he asked.

"Rum and coke," Maryah said.

An older man at the end of the bar looked up and raised his glass. Maryah nodded.

The bartender placed the drink in front of her. "Starting a tab?"

"It's that obvious?" Maryah asked and handed him a bill.

"Looks like you've had a long day," he said.

"Just flew in to go to my little brother's memorial service. The wake was tonight." Maryah stared at her glass.

"Hey, I'm sorry, that's rough," the bartender said.

"I hear that," the man on the end barstool said. "I'm Matt. I lost my brother four years ago. It doesn't get easier."

The bartender placed the money on the bar and slid it toward her. "It's on the house tonight."

"You're right. It doesn't get easier," Maryah nodded at them. "I lost my baby sister when we were kids. That still aches."

The bartender lined up three shot glasses and poured Jameson into them. He slid one over to her. Matt moved to the barstool beside her.

"What's your brother's name?" the bartender asked.

"Danny," Maryah choked.

The bartender raised his glass, as did Matt. "To Danny," they said.

Maryah picked up the shot glass and clinked it against theirs. "To Danny," she said. She held it up, then lowered it to the bar, untouched, next to the rum and coke. "Good night, gentlemen."

# 9

It was a few weeks after they had returned from Danny's funeral. She hadn't seen him since the funeral, further convincing her it had been a dream. Today was her first appointment with a grief counselor. She'd taken Connie's advice and made an appointment with Devon Lenier. She sat in the waiting room, feeling conspicuous and nervous.

A tall older gentleman popped in. He wore a tailored suit. "Maryah?"

She handed him a clipboard with her paperwork and followed him to his office, refusing the offer of coffee, tea, or water. She sat next to a box of tissues on a sofa.

"OK, tell me what brings you here," he began.

"Well," Maryah said, "I lost my little brother unexpectedly." She began crying at the mention of it. "I never expected him to go so young and first." She reached for a tissue and dabbed at her eyes.

"I see," Devon jotted something down on the notepad he held. "How long ago?"

"Just a few weeks," she muttered. "Somedays, I wake up and don't believe it happened."

"That's part of the grief process."

"I don't know," Maryah stated, watching Devon scribble more notes.

"The grief process?" Devon asked. "Or that your brother is gone?"

"Both."

Devon leaned back in the armchair and placed the pad face down on the coffee table. "The stages of grief are Denial, Anger, Bargaining, Depression, then Acceptance. Sometimes you can experience them all at once. You're still in the early phases."

"I think Danny was taken too soon," Maryah stated. "My husband and friend say it's due to guilt."

"Normal, and part of the process," Devon said. "Tell me about Danny?"

Maryah settled against the cushions and felt a momentary release. "He loved life, people. He could light up a room when he walked into it. He was generous, an awesome host, and a great brother. If I stayed closer to him, I would've seen this coming."

"How so?" Devon picked up the pad again.

"Give me a break," Danny said beside her on the sofa. "There's nothing you could've done. You've got the guilt thing down to a science."

"Sometimes, it seems like he's still here." Maryah turned to her brother, drawing in a sharp breath. She felt dizzy. It was happening again. "I feel light-headed. Could I get that cup of coffee?"

"Of course, dear." Devon looked concerned and sprung up. "This can be a reaction to grief and stress. Cream or black?"

"A little cream." Maryah gave a small smile. It *was* due to stress and grief.

"I thought you left me for good," she said.

Danny crossed his arms and sat back, stretching his legs out. "I'm here. You don't always see me."

"I'm glad you're here," she said.

"Why are you talking to this guy?" Danny asked.

"Lars and my friend thought it would help," Maryah said. "A neutral party to sort out things."

"Sometimes it helps to have that objectivity," he confirmed, "to help us move on."

"Have you talked to Giuseppe?" Maryah asked.

Danny nodded. "We have work to do."

"I'm ready," Maryah promised. If anything, she would

not fail him and try her darndest to make it up to him.

Devon returned, precluding further discussion. He picked up the pen and pad and gave her a long look. "Where should we start?"

~

MayBea rested in her doggie bed. It had been a few weeks since Maryah and Lars returned from the sad trip when she lost her brother. In that period, it was evident that Maryah was different. Goliath had said that despite the mighty pain, she was healing. He said we show our humans the way when they cannot see it.

Her work was coming to a close. Her people had changed toward each other. They were better together, kinder. Goliath told her she would be a young dog with no pain, able to play with her littermates. She would see her mother and those who have gone before her.

Since Maryah's return from the sad trip, MayBea observed Brother-Angel hovering nearby throughout the day. She wanted to let him know he was not alone, but Goliath warned her not to meddle.

Brother-Angel fretted a great deal, his concern for Maryah apparent. She liked him because of his goodness and how he brought it out in her.

MayBea had observed Brother-Angel lingering behind her, sighing when she fell into her human ways and smiling when she made progress. He was like her in many ways with his impulsiveness and gestures. Goliath said it was because they were siblings from the same parentage.

Today MayBea dozed in the sunshine. She did not ache

anymore in her daydreams as she played with her littermates.

"I know you can hear me."

MayBea opened her eyes to see Brother-Angel kneeling by her.

"You're stuck too?" he asked.

Goliath's warning echoed, but Brother-Angel had reached out to her.

"Uhh uhhmm." MayBea acknowledged him and struggled to sit up.

"We have much in common, dog," he said. "We need to help her before we can move on."

MayBea grunted.

"We've got our work cut out for us, dog. She's making progress, but my time here is running out."

Her time was also running out.

"You should take this one Home—too much pain. I can take care of my sister," Brother-Angel stated.

MayBea sat up. Goliath sat on her other side.

"I know it's not part of my assignment, but it seems you're running behind on getting this one Home," he said. "Something is keeping you here too? Can I help?"

MayBea lowered herself and curled up, trying to find the position where her body would ache the least. Goliath rested his chin on her head.

Brother-Angel stroked her, and with his touch came a tingling sensation. She rubbed her head against the back of his hand. The discomfort eased. At least Maryah would have Brother-Angel when she left.

"Who will I have when you're gone?" Brother-Angel asked.

How much he was like his sibling, needing comfort and reassurance.

"Sweet Dreams," he said.

Maryah sat in her home office. She picked up a framed photo on her desk. It showed Tommy, Danny, Melody, and herself, taken the summer before Melody died. Just four goofy kids playing on an August day. She ran a thumb over Melody's smiling face and then Danny's. To be able to take it back.

Almost midmorning, and she hadn't accomplished much. It had been six weeks since she'd last seen Danny and her first session with Devon.

She'd continued seeing the therapist and told him about seeing her brother. Devon didn't respond like she should be locked away in a padded room, but listened in a nonjudgmental way.

He indicated that it was one of the phases of grief called bargaining. Guilt and "what-if" questions were symptomatic of that. Was she trying to absolve her guilt?

Today she felt the pressure of MayBea against her feet beneath her desk. The dog's loud rhythmic snore comforted her.

"Danny, what am I going to do?" she whispered, tears running down her cheeks. "Oh, Mellie."

Not a day went by that she did not think of Melody. How old would she be today? Would she be married with children? Would she be taller than Maryah? Would she be a doctor, teacher, or artist? *If only, if only*, the catchphrase of her life.

MayBea snorted and sat up, jarring her thoughts.

"Want a biscuit?" she asked.

The dog waited, and Maryah headed to the kitchen.

"Here you go, sweetie," she said, holding the biscuit. She stopped at the sight of Danny Boy. Her heart leaped. "You're back!"

Standing against the wall in his customary garb, he nodded, reminding her of their father. Love and sadness filled her. Gosh, if she could have them both back.

The dog nuzzled her hand for the biscuit, trotted away with it, and dropped it before Danny. MayBea glanced up at him, then pawed at the biscuit.

"She can see you?" Maryah watched in awe. "What's she doing?"

"Even old dogs like to play now and then, sis." He bent down and pointed to the biscuit. "Get the biscuit."

MayBea pawed at it again, sending it a few inches across the floor.

"That wasn't me. I don't have control over mass," he reassured. "Smart dog, she made up this game." He pointed to the biscuit again. "Get it, girl. It's all yours."

The dog barked and pawed the biscuit, launching it a few more inches. MayBea trotted over, picked it up, and chewed it. She sauntered back and collapsed under the desk, asleep in seconds.

"Guess we let that cat out of the bag. Get it 'cat' out of the bag, not dog?" Danny laughed—another Giancano habit, laughing at their own jokes.

Lord, it was good to hear him laugh. She could almost

believe that he was alive. Maryah smiled at the oddity that her dog could see the apparition of her brother.

"Where have you been?" she wondered.

"Time is different here. It's not like hours or days," Danny said.

"I need you, Brother. I never realized how much until I lost you," Maryah said.

"You were wondering about her?" Danny asked.

Her stomach fell. Mellie. Had he heard her? Her cheeks felt warm. "The rules," she whispered, acknowledging that she knew not to ask about any of their departed family.

"Wow, you're trying to follow the rules for once." He paused. "You called her name today."

"Melody." She swallowed hard. MayBea pressed against her legs. "I failed you both."

"You didn't fail either of us." Danny folded his arms and studied her. "You were an excellent big sister."

"I shouldn't have given her my skates," she stated in a monotone. She'd said it, what she mulled over every day.

"We were kids, Maryah." Danny bent to pat MayBea. "Let. It. Go."

"But when I laced up the skates," Maryah began. Her heart pounded. She reached for her water bottle and took a slug. No alcohol to hide behind.

He nodded and ran a hand over MayBea.

"I left the lacing loose. I knew since my skates would be too big, she'd stumble and not want to bother skating," Maryah blurted. Ouch, the horrible truth she'd never spoken. "It's my fault Mellie slipped and fell in. I deliberately left the skate binding loose."

Her words hung in the air between them. Danny stood up and crossed his arms.

"All this time," he said, "that's a lot of baggage to carry."

"I wish it had been me." She swallowed hard. "I'd give anything to have you back instead of me."

"Remember when you had a nature call?" Danny ran a hand through his hair. "Mellie kept saying 'wee-wee' over and over?"

Maryah nodded.

"Before Mellie stood up, I could see the skates were too loose, so I retied them for her," Danny said.

The blood thumped in her ears. Maryah blinked twice and trembled.

"It was her time," Danny said. "It wasn't your fault."

Maryah sat across from Devon at their next appointment. She'd seen him weekly for two months.

"How are things going?" he began.

"It's still strange, walking through the feelings and fear," Maryah said. "I never realized how much I used alcohol to insulate myself from everything."

"To stop drinking is one hurdle," Devon said. "Learning to navigate life without it is something else. Are you going to meetings?"

"Almost every day," she said. "You think once you quit drinking, then everything is OK. But life still has its problems."

"What's on your mind?" Devon asked.

"Danny isn't the only sibling I failed," Maryah whimpered. "There was my baby sister, Melody."

"Yes, you've mentioned she fell through the ice when you were kids," Devon said. "How old were you when it happened?"

"Nine," she said. "Mellie was six, and I was in charge."

"That's a lot of responsibility for a nine-year-old, don't you think?" Devon reasoned.

"Maybe," she agreed. "She was the cutest but could be stubborn. I wish I'd said no and kept her off the ice."

"She may have gone anyway. Is there anyone else who holds you responsible?" Devon wondered. "Or is it just you?"

"Danny said it's not my fault," she whispered. A relief of sorts washed over her.

"Then what?" Devon prompted.

"All this time, I thought it was me," she said.

"When we can finally feel the feelings and let go of guilt and shame, we can begin the healing process."

Maryah let out a deep breath. All those years ago, on the pond, Melody wanted to be like her big sister and ice skate. Tears began rolling down her cheeks. She lowered her face to her hands and wept.

# 10

The day after her appointment with Devon, Maryah sat on the sofa clutching a tissue and watched MayBea in a restless sleep in her doggie bed.

Lars walked into the room and sat beside her. He held her hand. “The vet tech will be here later,” he said. “Want me to call Connie?”

She shook her head. “I’ll talk to her.” This she must do herself.

He picked up the phone and handed it to her. Maryah held it and waited for it to ring. She began weeping at the sound of Connie’s voice.

“I think it’s time for MayBea,” Maryah said. “She’s not eating or drinking. She threw up this morning. The vet’s coming later.”

“Honey, you knew this day would come,” Connie responded. “It’s the hardest day of every pet owner’s life.”

“It’s so hard,” Maryah wept. “I want you here to be sure.”

“I’m on my way,” Connie replied.

Maryah was sitting on the floor beside MayBea's doggie bed when she heard Lars greet Connie in the kitchen. Maryah stood to hug her when they entered the room.

"I'm sorry," Connie said. "Are you OK?"

"My heart is breaking," Maryah sobbed.

Connie looked between Lars and Maryah and held their hands in hers. "The most important thing you have is each other. Never forget it."

Maryah nodded, then was pulled into an embrace with Connie and Lars.

"Thank you," she murmured.

MayBea sat up and snorted. Maryah observed as the dog stood and walked to Connie.

"She's doing better now. I almost wonder if it's the right decision," Maryah wondered.

Lars nodded. "If she's doing better, perhaps we have more time."

Connie kneeled and ran a hand over the dog. "Let me have a few minutes with her," she said.

Lars wrapped an arm around her shoulders and led Maryah toward the kitchen. "I'll make us some tea," he said.

Maryah leaned against him and swallowed hard. "Thank you."

MayBea breathed hard and struggled to sit up when Connie entered the room. Maryah and Lars and not been alone in their vigil. Brother-Angel and Goliath had also been there. She felt a soft, feathery touch when Goliath leaned against her. The pain eased.

Connie kneeled and caressed her head. "Oh, my sweet girl," she whispered. "I held you when you took your first breath."

MayBea grunted at Goliath. "Do what you came for, then your work here is finished too."

Goliath raised his chin and leaned against Connie's shoulder.

MayBea sat between them. "Yes, help her."

Connie sat cross-legged, one hand on MayBea, then closed her eyes. The sound of the kettle shrilled from the kitchen.

"Oh, my poor boy, what you endured," she uttered.

*Forgive and let it go. Love never dies. That's what I remember from my time with you, the love.*

Although Goliath made no sound, MayBea understood his message to Connie.

Connie opened her eyes and stared at where Goliath sat, his head resting on her shoulder. She reached out to stroke him, but then he was gone.

MayBea lowered herself to her bed.

Connie glanced up to where Maryah stood, holding two cups of tea.

"Are you OK?" Maryah asked.

Connie nodded and struggled to stand.

"MayBea's doing better," Maryah repeated. "I think we can wait."

Connie shook her head. "I'm sorry, dear. It's time. MayBea is ready, and she won't be alone. Love lives on," she said and began sobbing.

Maryah sat beside her.

"He was such a good boy," Connie said. "He forgave

me."

"Who?" Maryah sounded confused.

"Goliath," Connie replied.

Goliath was back beside the doggie bed and lifted his head at the mention of his name.

Connie put a hand on her chest and exhaled. "He'll take care of our darling when she leaves."

"Uhh, uhhmm." MayBea tried to tell them before exhaustion overtook her. "Goliath will take care of me."

MayBea tried to grunt and tell Maryah, "It's time."

"Oh, my darling MayBea," Maryah cried.

MayBea opened her eyes and tried to sit up. Maryah kissed and hugged her. Lars wrapped his arms around them both. Connie stood behind them, Goliath beside her.

Brother-Angel kneeled behind his sister, a hand on her shoulder.

Maryah sobbed into her fur. "I will love you forever."

MayBea rested her head against Maryah. Together with Brother-Angel, they had shown Maryah beyond the walls she built around herself. How fortunate to be loved this much.

MayBea tried but could not make a sound. Did Maryah understand that she would always be with her? Always.

The vet tech approached, and Goliath moved closer. MayBea felt a brief burning sensation. She knew Maryah's heart was breaking. They were bound by love.

"It's goodbye but not farewell," Brother-Angel said.

# 11

It had been a few weeks since MayBea's passing. By working with Devon, Maryah found that despite the awful ache in her heart, she was coping. She went to the twelve-step meetings almost daily.

MayBea's doggie beds, crate, and toys remained throughout the house. She couldn't bear to put them away. Sometimes, sitting at her desk, she imagined feeling the gentle nuzzle of MayBea against her. More than once, she thought she'd spotted her beloved pet in a familiar spot.

Lars had been cooking dinner for them the past few weeks, getting home earlier. He tried to fill the gap. The protective fortress she'd built around herself had melted. She recalled Giuseppe telling her she needed to work on forgiveness.

She stared at her reflection in the bathroom mirror. Her eyes were the same green as Melody's, her hair the same brown as Danny's. She pointed and began to cry and laugh alternately. All this time, like Dorothy and the ruby slippers, right before her. If this didn't prove she should be committed, then nothing would.

"I forgive you," she whispered.

In the next instant, Danny Boy stood beside her. She drew in a sharp breath. Joy filled her. She hadn't seen him in weeks.

"Took you long enough." He sighed.

She held his gaze in the mirror. In the past, she'd used alcohol to avoid confrontation. Now she tried to live by the principles that had governed Danny's life. Honesty. Forgiveness. Facing your fears.

"Do you forgive me?" she asked. The next instant, they were on the same beach she'd had been on with Giuseppe. The tide was coming in.

"Good, at least you're not being a weasel and avoiding the truth," Danny commented. "Giuseppe made the right choice. You weren't ready."

"They took you instead of me," she uttered. "How can you forgive me?"

"Haven't you learned? Let go of the regrets." He sounded exasperated, but smiled. "You're coming along, sis. Things might be different if today was your return date."

Only Danny would tease about such a serious thing. Maryah smiled back. "But Danny, you'd still be gone," she whispered.

"Gosh, Maryah, you hang on to everything. Let it go."

"I'll try," she promised.

"Remember, sis, who we are: vocal, Irish, Italian, caring, meddlesome, and family." Danny reached to mess up her hair as he would when they were kids, but the wind picked up and blew her hair awry.

A wave of understanding washed over her. "You're leaving me forever." She raised her voice, no longer disguising the panic and anguish. "It's the real goodbye until it's my turn."

"Yeah, Maryah, it is. You'll be fine." He turned and walked down the beach.

She ran to keep up with his long-legged stride. She'd miss him popping up in her life whenever he felt necessary. He didn't seem to be reading her thoughts anymore. "Danny, can you visit now and then?"

"My assignment is complete," he said. "That dog of yours is doggone special. Doggone, get it? You're fortunate to be loved like that."

"You've seen her?" She found herself smiling despite her sadness.

He nodded.

"I miss her so," her voice broke. The rawness of his leaving walloped her. "Please stay."

He stopped and turned to her, back to the sun, casting a long shadow. "Goodbye and letting go are the hardest things we do."

"I'm going to miss you," she cried.

"Be a beacon for my wife and daughter. Tell them that love is what matters in the end." He flashed a brilliant smile.

When he gave her his wonderful, charming smile, she knew it would be the last she'd see of him in this world, dreams or not. Desperate, afraid, deserted, she screamed. "Don't go. If you leave, who will help me?"

The light around Danny brightened. "We're here, ready to listen and help. I love you, sis."

He walked on, gliding over the rocks as the surf rolled in. The sun was setting at a frantic pace. The tide made it impossible for her to scale the rocks that separated them.

He stood at the highest point on the jagged rocks and faced her. He held out something in his arms. It was a puppy with similar markings to MayBea.

The sky around him became luminescent, the sun blinding her. Then it became still and calm, the tide coming in a gentle, rhythmic motion. The last rays of sunlight hung on the horizon.

Danny Boy had gone Home. Maryah was left behind.

She awoke at home, head resting on her desk. The reality of Danny's death stung hard and fresh. No more visits from him. The image of him holding MayBea and walking into the distance played in her mind. The dog's snoring no longer filled the room; the ticking of the wall clock was the only sound. Pangs of grief gripped her. She fell to her knees, long, hard sobs echoing.

"I don't care whose angel you are, Giuseppe. You screwed up. Danny was *my* angel. Give him back," she screamed. "I hate you."

She lay curled on the rug and cried herself out. Her body ached, and her eyes stung. She struggled to stand.

He sat in the office chair and spun around. His fists clenched, arms by his side. If an angel could look infuriated, then it was Giuseppe.

Maryah folded her arms and glared.

"Hate?" Giuseppe broke the silent tug of war between them.

"You and Antonio messed up. Danny was doing a fine job. I want him back," she stated.

"Hate?" he repeated.

"I'm sorry. How about not happy with either one of you?" she offered.

He shook his head and stared at the wall behind her.

They were back to the standoff, but Maryah held her ground. It was their fault. "I want him back."

"You don't get to choose. We cannot select the subjects we serve." Giuseppe snapped. "It has not been easy for Antonio. Why do you think Danny's help was enlisted? This is the thanks we get?"

"It was my turn," she whispered. "Make Danny my guardian angel."

Giuseppe rose and loomed over her. Goodness, he was taller than her father. She took a step back.

"Ah, it is as if you have learned nothing." He despaired.

"Your brother was much advanced for his time. You were not."

"I realize that guilt, self-centeredness, and being unforgiving got me into this mess," Maryah retorted.

"Ah, so you have learned something." Giuseppe regarded her with an unreadable expression.

"If I've learned anything, it's been from Danny. He forgave me despite it all," she said. "If we agree on anything, it's that he was extraordinary. It breaks my heart to lose him once more."

"We must continue to work on forgiveness, kindness, and love," Giuseppe said in a softer tone.

"I bet I have a long way to go," she muttered.

"Not as much as the stubborn, angry woman from a few months ago," Giuseppe responded. "Danny Boy showed you the way. The Powers Above Us were most impressed. They have other assignments for him."

"What if I fail? I may need Danny Boy to help me along the way," Maryah reasoned.

Giuseppe smiled. "You will fail at times because you are human. Look at Antonio and me. We're Certified Angels, and we made a mistake."

"Then were you forgiven?"

He gave a huge smile that she knew she would not see in her human world. "Danny Boy, taken before his time, forgave us all," he said. "He is one in a million and has gone to a higher place. We are most fortunate for knowing him."

"I'm fortunate to have him and you," she whispered. She had been privileged to savor the grace and light of Danny's initial angel-in-training days. He'd gone beyond normal angel status at an accelerated rate due to his incredible capacity to forgive and love.

"Yes, indeed," Giuseppe replied.

"But his wife and daughter? How do I explain this to them?"

"You can't," Giuseppe replied in his no-frills manner. "Share what Danny Boy taught you. Love and forgiveness prevail in the face of fear and anger."

"It's goodbye to you and Danny. Too much for one afternoon." She smiled despite her sadness. He was a delightful mix of her father and Danny in the familiar dysfunctional Giancano way.

"Ah, but it's not farewell. Talk to us whenever you choose. We always listen."

"It's not the same." She brushed away a tear.

Giuseppe reached out and touched her cheek. His hand had the same leathery, callused touch as her father's.

She held his hand, closed her eyes, breathed hard, and let the tears fall.

"The hard part for you, my child, is waiting for the answer," he said. "Listen with your heart."

He was gone when she opened her eyes, her hand pressed against her cheek.

# 12

Maryah continued to see Devon biweekly. Sometimes she cried simultaneously about losing her sister, brother, and pet. She'd shared that Danny's final visit was like reliving the initial trauma of his death.

"You're processing your emotions and learning to accept," Devon explained.

"I never realized I'd walled myself away and held so much in," she told him.

Between his encouragement, Danny's prodding, and Giuseppe's nudging, she'd learned to allow herself to be vulnerable with those dearest to her.

Another time, Connie opened up to her. "When I hugged MayBea goodbye, I released the hurt and anger I had at my father," she shared. "I know he had dark secrets from his past that contributed to his drinking."

"Letting go is the hardest thing we do," Maryah responded. "Danny taught me that includes anger, bitterness, and regret. It holds your heart prisoner." She no longer focused on the regrets of her life and tried to be present in the moment.

Today she sat on the deck and gazed at MayBea's favorite pine tree to nap under. She closed her eyes, yearning to hear MayBea's snoring. She imagined Danny standing behind her in the same stance as their father. It would've been Danny's birthday.

"You're the best brother and have an amazing family," she said. "They are your legacy. I'm getting to know them better." Maryah paused, longing for his impatient sigh at the tribute. "I feel like I got to know you better after you became my angel. It must've been a difficult first assignment. You forgave me when I couldn't forgive myself. Thank you."

She imagined him nodding in agreement. The Giancanos were a bunch of hams, Danny not being the least among them. Nothing followed, no appearance of him, not even a reprimanding visit from Giuseppe.

"Just one little sigh or whisper?" she pleaded.

*Listen with your heart*, Giuseppe had said.

She'd told Giuseppe she might write about it. But where to start? It wasn't just her story and that of Danny, the reluctant angel. There was MayBea and the joy she brought.

Lars pulled into the driveway. He wasn't due home for a few hours. She hurried into the house.

"What's wrong?" she asked when he entered the kitchen.

He kissed her cheek. "My little worrier."

"Why are you home early?" she persisted.

"Not glad to see me?"

"Yes, but you never break your routine," she continued. "You're up to something."

"I figured you'd need cheering up today," he said.

"You remembered," Maryah whispered.

"Sit," Lars commanded, pointing to a kitchen table chair.

"You brought dinner?" she asked. "I hope it's Italian."

"Sit and be patient," he said.

Maryah's stomach growled. It had been fantastic to have him take over the evening meal preparation. Perhaps a delicious lasagna from Bella Mia's awaited her.

The garage door to the kitchen opened, but she resisted the urge to turn around. She didn't smell pasta or much of anything.

"Cover your eyes," Lars ordered.

"OK, OK," she muttered.

"Open your eyes," he said.

A brindle and white puppy with a brown patch near one eye sat on the table. The puppy began to chew on a napkin. Maryah sat speechless.

"Meet Sparkle," he said. "She's from Connie's most recent litter."

"I don't know." Maryah groaned. "It's too soon."

"The dog is ours," Lars said. "Connie won't take her back."

"Rotten," Maryah said. "You're in cahoots."

Sparkle teetered close to the edge of the table. Maryah gathered up the puppy.

Lars sat down and patted Sparkle. "She's pretty spunky."

"A puppy is lots of work," Maryah whimpered, leaning against him. "I love you. Thank you."

~

She'd been scared on the car ride over with the man. She missed her mama and the other dogs. The woman was soft, and Sparkle liked how she smelled.

A bulldog sat on the floor and leaned against the woman. Sparkle raised her head and barked at her new friend. The woman hugged her and put her down. Sparkle no longer felt afraid.

The angel bulldog leaned close and licked her ear. "Welcome, little one. Welcome home."

**-END-**

# ACKNOWLEDGMENTS

Writing this book was far harder than I imagined but worth the effort. It That it has come together in a story that can be told is due to the folks listed below. It takes a village.

My initial quest found Jessica Snyder of HEA Author Services, thank you for listening and leading me to Kimberly Hunt of the Revision Division. I am indebted to Kimberly for your editorial skill and guiding me through rewrites. This project would not have come to fruition without you. Many thanks to Robin Phillips and the team at Author Help UK for providing professional support and guidance in publishing.

My dear friend, Laura Mullen, provided amazing feedback and would be a heck of an editor if she chose. I'm grateful for your help and friendship. Thank you to my beta reader on many projects, Rachel Wilson. I appreciate the time and effort.

My support includes my better half, Bruce, I appreciate your patience and understanding when I was hiding down the writing rabbit-hole. I must mention Maryellen, who has supported me through every endeavor in life, this was no different. There were times I wanted to give up and Annie encouraged me not to. I want to thank Birgit and Othella for listening when I needed to share.

My dear sister-in-law, Missy, an amazing author in her own right (Lauren Giordano), provided support, comfort and feedback. Thank you for allowing me to use photos of Danny for the illustrations and cover.

# ABOUT THE AUTHOR

Maria McShane has always had a vivid imagination and has been writing ever since she could remember. Growing up in an old colonial home in New England, across from an old cemetery, was the beginning of inspiration for her stories. As much as the cemetery scared her, it fired her creativity and served as inspiration for her stories.

She loves hiking, the Red Sox, and if you haven't guessed, English Bulldogs. She lives in the Southwestern United States with her husband. She's hoping to retire and explore the countryside with her husband in an RV and a bulldog when the right one finds her.

She's written many short stories over the years and a collection is her next endeavor.

The Reluctant Angel is her debut novel.

Made in the USA
Middletown, DE
09 July 2024